Jack's
Endless· Summer

Martyn Hobbs

About this Book

For the Student

🎧 Listen to all of the story and do some activities on your Audio CD
💬 Talk about the story
beat• When you see the blue dot you can check the word in the glossary
🅚 Prepare for Cambridge English: Key (KET) for Schools

For the Teacher

 A state-of-the-art interactive learning environment with 1000s of free online self-correcting activities for your chosen readers.

Go to our Readers Resource site for information on using readers and downloadable Resource Sheets, photocopiable Worksheets and Answer Keys. Plus free sample tracks from the story.

www.helblingreaders.com

For lots of great ideas on using Graded Readers consult Reading Matters, the Teacher's Guide to using Helbling Readers.

Level 1 Structures

Present simple of *be*	*A / an*
Have got	*The*
There is / there are	Subject pronouns
Present Simple	Object pronouns
Can (ability and permission)	Plural nouns
Present Continuous	Countable and uncountable nouns
	Some / any
Like / love / hate / don't like doing	
Imperatives	Adjectives
Short answers	Possessive adjectives
Who? What? Where? What colour?	Possessive *'s*
How much? How many?	Demonstrative adjectives and pronouns
Adverbs of frequency	*very*

NEW for Helbling Readers

Helbling Readers e-zone is the brand new state-of-the-art easy-to-use interactive learning environment from Helbling Languages. Each book has its own set of online interactive self-correcting cyber homework activities containing a range of reading comprehension, vocabulary, listening comprehension, grammar and exam preparation exercises.

Students test their language skills in a stimulating interactive environment. All activities can be attempted as many times as necessary and full results and feedback are given as soon as the deadline has been reached. Single student access is also available.

Teachers register free of charge to set up classes and assign individual and class homework sets. Results are provided automatically once the deadline has been reached and detailed reports on performance are available at a click.

1000s of free online interactive activities now available.

www.helbling-ezone.com

Contents

Before Reading 6
Jack's Endless Summer 11
After Reading 54
Glossary 62

Before Reading

1 Look at the picture and answer the questions on pages 8 and 9.

Jack's room

Before Reading

Before Reading

1 Label Jack's room on page 6 with the words below.

   a) sunglasses   b) curtains   c) rocket
   d) cap   e) catapult   f) pillow

2 Label Jack's back garden on page 7 with the words below.

   a) hawk   b) shadow   c) claws
   d) shed   e) feather   f) wing
   g) eye   h) beak

3 Look at the pictures and discuss the questions.

Jack's room
- How does Jack feel?
- What is the weather like?
- What time of the year is it?
- Where are his friends?

Jack's back garden
- What is Jack looking at?
- How does Jack feel?
- Why do you think he feels like this?

4 All these things in the pictures are important in the story. Why are they important? Can you guess? In groups write a scenario. In your scenario try to include lots of the words from Exercises 1 and 2. Then tell the class. Choose the best scenario.

Before Reading

5 Listen and match the names with the pictures.

> Tareq   Jack   Mum   Damian   Jim   Holly

a) ....   b) ....   c) ....

d) ....   e) ....   f) ....

6 Answer the questions.

My summer holidays

- How long are your summer holidays?
- What do you usually do?
- How often do you see your school friends?
- How do you feel during the holidays?
- Are you sometimes bored? Why?

7 Compare your answers to Exercise 6 in groups.

Jack's Endless Summer

Some summers never end.
Every day is the same. It is hot before the sun rises. It is hot after the sun falls.
And between morning and night, when the sun burns in the sky...
birds stop singing...
dogs stop barking...
cats stop creeping...
fish stop swimming...
and even time seems to stop.

You look at your watch. You study the clock. You check your mobile phone. You wait and wait for a minute to pass. But it is hot. Very hot. And it seems to be three o'clock forever.

Jack lies on his bed in his room. His window is open but his curtains are closed, to keep out the bright sunshine. His curtains don't move. There isn't a breath of air. The world is hot and still.

Jack lies on his bed in the dim• quiet of his bedroom. He is only wearing shorts and a T-shirt but his body feels heavy and sticky• and hot. His bed feels hot, too. And his pillow is like a heater.

His lifts a heavy hand and looks at his mobile. There are three new messages. There are people in the world with the energy to send text messages. But not here. Not in Westbourne on this hot summer day.

Jack's Endless Summer

Who are the messages from?
He clicks on the first one. It is from Zadie.

Hey Jack,
How are you? What are you doing? I'm lying on the beach drinking a long cold fruit juice with loads• of ice. The sun's shining but it isn't too hot – there's a beautiful cool breeze• coming from the sea. The water here is fantastic. I go swimming every day and sometimes I go surfing. It's amazing! And every morning I go for a really long run on the beach. It's brilliant here. I don't want to come home. I hope you're having a great summer too!
Z xxx

The second message is from David.

Hi Jack,
I'm staying with my aunt up here in Edinburgh. It's my first time in Scotland, and it's fantastic! The buildings are tall and there are lots of narrow• streets and strange little squares. I'm staying on the top floor• of a building• in the centre of the city. I can see for miles!

I'm reading lots of books by a great Edinburgh writer – Robert Louis Stevenson. I love *Treasure Island*. But *Doctor Jekyll and Mister Hyde* is my favourite. It is a very scary story! So, what am I doing every evening? I'm writing a frightening story with a horrible character called 'The Scarecrow'. He is tall and thin and his skin is grey. He only comes out at night. You can read it when I come home!
See you soon,
David

Jack's Endless Summer

The third message is from Holly.

Hello Jack

This is the best holiday ever. Pity• it's nearly over. We're staying in a big wooden chalet high up in the mountains. It's so beautiful here. The mountains are amazing – there's snow on some of them! Every day I go for a long walk and take photos of all the wild flowers. Sometimes I make short video films on my mobile. Hope you're happy in Westbourne. I hear it's hot. It's cool here at night and I have to sleep under a lovely warm blanket!
Holly xxxxx

Jack shakes his head. His friends are so lucky!
He always meets his gang in the park in the afternoon. He gets up and looks for his cap and sunglasses. He can't see them. Maybe they are downstairs. So he picks up• his bag and leaves his room.

15

Jack's Endless Summer

Jack bangs the front door shut.
Nemo, the neighbour's cat, is lying on the garden wall. He opens his one eye and watches Jack walk down the path towards him.
'How are you today, Nemo?' Jack asks.
Nemo doesn't reply. He closes his one eye again.
Jack walks down the road. It is so hot. He can smell the tarmac•. The trees look tired and heavy in the sunshine. Their leaves are covered in grey summer dust•.
And even here, outside, there is no air.
So Jack heads towards• the park. He is walking along the road when he hears a noise...

WSSSSSSSSS....!
The noise is coming closer...

WSSSSSSSSSSSSSSS!
A small dark shape flies past his head and hits a plastic dustbin with a loud

CRRRACCCCKKKK!!!!!!!!

Jack's Endless Summer

Jack watches a hard rubber ball bounce• on the pavement and then roll away across the road.
And then he hears laughter.
He turns around quickly and sees four boys running away. One of them is tall with short red hair and he is holding... what is that? Then Jack understands. It's a catapult.
Jack immediately looks for the ball. He can throw it at the boys. There it is! It's lying in the gutter•. He runs towards the ball without looking.
'Be careful!' a woman shouts loudly – and a bicycle cycles past him.
Jack looks for the boys.
He can't see them now. He is on his own and the world is silent and still again.

19

In the park, Jack walks slowly to a tall old tree. His dark shadow moves silently next to him. He is feeling angry and he is still thinking about the boy with the catapult. Who is he? Jack doesn't know him. He is probably new to the area. Another enemy•, Jack thinks, with another gang.

When he gets to the tree he lies down in the shadow. He rubs his eyes. He feels hot and tired and annoyed•. He looks across the dry yellow grass. Two girls are throwing a Frisbee. An old man is walking his dog. But where are his friends Liam and Tareq? He gets out his mobile and sends Liam a text.

where RU• Liam?
Jack

Then Jack lies on his back, rests his head on his bag, and looks up into the leaves. The sun is shining brightly up above but the leaves make a sparkling• green screen. Are they moving? Are they still? He can't decide. But some are light and others dark. His eyes grow heavy. He looks up and he imagines he is a large heavy shark• swimming under the sea. He is swimming in warm water. He is silent and dangerous and...

He hears a voice call out, 'Damian, come on!'

Jack ignores• it. It isn't Liam or Tareq.

He feels the hard dry ground under him. He isn't a shark now. He can feel the huge round planet under his head and back and legs. The planet is turning in infinite space. He can feel it turning beneath him. And the sky up above is infinite. Space is infinite...

Jack's Endless Summer

Jack looks up through half-closed eyes at the blue sky.
He imagines his body floating• up from the earth. What can stop him? Gravity? No. He doesn't have any weight. He is like a feather. He is light and he is floating up into the blue sky.
Now he is floating in air, turning slowly, gently. He is slowly spinning• with the planet, spinning in space.
The world is far below him. The houses are small, the cars are toys, the people are insects.
Then he hears a cry.
What is it?
He hears it again. It is loud, like a child, but different. It's a strange sound.
Then he can feel something moving around him. It is above him, then below him...
Jack's eyes suddenly open. Where is he? He sees the leaves above him. He isn't floating in the air. He is lying on the ground.
He looks at his mobile. There is a text message from Liam.

CU• at the pool

The outdoor pool is the best place to be on a hot summer day.
Liam and Tareq are good swimmers. They are racing up and down the pool. Jack joins them at the beginning, but he stops after the first length•. He can swim but he isn't a strong swimmer. Jack lies on his back and floats. He feels cool and relaxed now.

Jack is looking up at the endless blue sky when he hears that cry again. The cry is like a child, but it isn't a child. And for a moment he sees a dark shape, like a dark angel. It is circling high in the sky, near the sun. But then he hears Tareq shout out:

'Look out, Jack!'

Jack raises his head quickly. But something crashes into the water next to him. There's an explosion of water. It goes into his eyes and mouth and he starts coughing•.

Jack's Endless Summer

The pool attendant• blows his whistle• loudly. Then he shouts at a boy standing next to Jack in the water.
'Hey, Damian, stop that!'
Damian? It's that name again.
Jack wipes• the water from his eyes and sees a boy with short red hair. The boy is smiling but it isn't a friendly smile. It is the boy with the catapult. Damian. So that's his name.
'Sorry!' Damian says. He doesn't mean it•. He swims over to his three friends.
The pool attendant looks down at Jack.
'Are you all right?' he asks. He isn't really interested. He just wants a quiet life.
Jack nods• and the pool attendant returns to his chair.
Jack looks at the four boys sitting on the edge• of the pool. They are chatting and laughing and pointing at him.
Jack turns away and swims to the other side.

That evening, while Jack and Jim are eating pizzas in front of the TV, Jim asks:
'Can you fix my rocket?'
Jack is sorry about the morning's accident. He likes his little brother.
'Sure,' Jack says. 'Don't worry. I can fix it after dinner.'
Later, after the quizzes and sport and soaps•, Jack takes the broken rocket up to his room. But he can't repair it. He wants to repair• it, but he is too hot. It's too hot to think. And it's too hot to sleep.
So Jack sits by the open window, looking out. Music is playing in the distance. There's a party in the next street. Some people are singing and laughing. He hears a neighbour shout, 'Be quiet!' The music stays quiet for perhaps ten minutes... then it gets loud again. And all over Westbourne, people are tired and hot and unable to sleep.

Jack's Endless Summer

Jack thinks about Damian. He can see his face and short red hair. And he can remember his annoying smile.
Jack imagines• a secret ambush•. He imagines throwing plastic bags full of water at Damian. He imagines a giant catapult throwing stones and dirt and rubbish all over his new enemy.
But then he sees the moon. It is like a circle of ice. On the moon the air is lovely and cold. It is a cold empty place.
A dark shape moves across its white surface. It moves slowly and silently. It is flying between the earth and the moon, far above the noise and the terrible heat. It is drifting• on its big cool wings. Is it an owl•? No. He hears its cry again, for the third time that day.
It is a hawk. It circles in the night sky, again and again.
Jack watches it closely. It is beautiful, peaceful, magical.
In the morning, he wakes up on the floor beneath the open window.

What day is it today? Tuesday? Wednesday?
Jack doesn't know. Every day is the same. And every evening.
He meets Liam and Tareq as usual. They don't know what to do.
'What can we do?'
'I don't know.'
'I don't want to play computer games.'
'Or watch TV.'
'Or play football.'
'Or stay inside.'
'Or stay outside.'
'I'm tired.'
'I'm bored.'
'What about Knock Down Ginger?' suggests Liam.
'What's that?' asks Tareq.
'It's an old game,' replies Liam and he explains the rules.
Tareq and Jack hide behind a parked car. Liam rings a doorbell• then runs away and joins them. They wait and watch a man open his front door. The man looks around, walks down the path and looks along the road. First left, then right, then left again. He sees nobody. So he shakes his head and walks back into his house.
Jack and his gang laugh quietly.

Jack's Endless Summer

The game is very funny the first few times. Tareq tries it, then Jack, then Liam again. The same thing happens again and again. People open their front doors and are surprised to see nobody there. Sometimes they check their doorbells. Other times they shake their heads, looking annoyed.
Then Tareq does it a second time. He rings the doorbell and hides. After a long pause, an old lady opens the door. She is confused when nobody is there. She goes back inside her house and closes the door. It doesn't seem very funny anymore.
'It's your turn next,' says Liam to Jack. 'Let's play one last time.'
Jack chooses a house. It is big with a long front garden. The lights are on inside.
'OK, I'm going in,' Jack says to his mates•. Then he opens the garden gate and walks quickly along the path.

Jack's Endless Summer

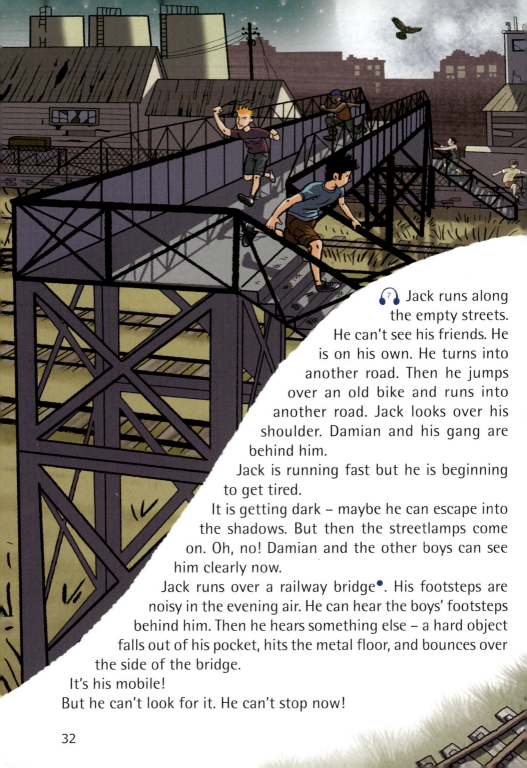

🎧 Jack runs along the empty streets. He can't see his friends. He is on his own. He turns into another road. Then he jumps over an old bike and runs into another road. Jack looks over his shoulder. Damian and his gang are behind him.

Jack is running fast but he is beginning to get tired.

It is getting dark – maybe he can escape into the shadows. But then the streetlamps come on. Oh, no! Damian and the other boys can see him clearly now.

Jack runs over a railway bridge•. His footsteps are noisy in the evening air. He can hear the boys' footsteps behind him. Then he hears something else – a hard object falls out of his pocket, hits the metal floor, and bounces over the side of the bridge.

It's his mobile!
But he can't look for it. He can't stop now!

32

Jack's Endless Summer

Jack runs down the metal steps on the other side of the bridge. There are no streetlights and it is very dark. He runs over small black stones and jumps over old railway lines. The long shiny tracks curve into the distance. He runs past old broken train carriages and through tall grass and weeds•. Jack can hear the boys' voices. They are looking for him in the dark!
He is tired and out of breath and the boys are getting closer. Jack runs behind a train carriage and hides. He can hear them talking.
'Where is he?'
'Can you see him?'
'Come on, come on out!' Damian shouts.
Jack doesn't move.

The boys call out again and again.
'Come out, mate! Let's see your stupid face!'
They look for Jack for a few minutes but they soon get bored.
'Forget it. He's not here.'
They walk back towards the bridge. The moon is high in the sky now. The boys look up. There is a dark shape circling above their heads in the light of the moon. It isn't high up. They can see its beak. Perhaps they can even see its eyes.
'Hey, man, can you see that?'
'It's a giant bird.'
'Hang on•, I've got an idea,' says Damian.
He bends down• and picks up a stone. Then he takes his catapult out of his pocket.
'Watch this.'

Jack's Endless Summer

He puts the stone into the catapult, and points it at the bird. Jack can see all this. He wants to stop them – he wants to shout out 'NO!' – but what can he do? He looks in horror as Damian fires• the stone into the air... and he hits the hawk! He hits the hawk! It makes no noise, but it suddenly drops three or four metres, then swoops• down low across the ground.

'Ha ha! Good shot•, Damian!'

'First time lucky!'

'No, I'm not lucky. I'm Robin Hood!'

They all think this is funny and have a good laugh.

'Come on,' Damian says, 'let's go back to my house. I'm hungry.'

So the boys climb up the steps again and cross the bridge. Jack comes out from behind the carriage. In the moonlight he can see quite clearly, but he can't see the hawk. Is it in the air? Is it on the ground?

He walks up and down. He looks under the old train carriages, he looks behind big bushes•. But he can't see the bird.
He hears an owl hoot•. It's getting late. Then he sees something on the railway track at his feet. He bends down and examines it. It is a beautiful long brown feather. A hawk's feather.
He follows the track and sees two more feathers. He stops and listens. Nothing. Then he hears a soft strange sound. Where is it coming from? He walks towards the sound and sees a wooden box. The hawk is lying behind the box.
It looks up at him and screeches•.
Jack can see the bird is in pain•. One of its wings is touching the ground. Its eyes look frightened. Its beak is hard and sharp.
'What can I do?' asks Jack. 'How can I help you?'
Then he makes a decision.

Jack's Endless Summer

There is only one thing he can do.
He takes off his T-shirt and he wraps• it carefully round the hawk. The hawk is frightened and it tries to escape. It tries to attack Jack with its beak and claws, but Jack is brave. He puts his T-shirt round the hawk like a blanket. It can't attack him now. Then he picks it up and carries it home.
Ten minutes later, Jack is walking through the streets under the streetlamps. Some young men see him and call out, 'What's under your T-shirt, mate?' Jack doesn't reply. He keeps on walking.
After half an hour he has a terrible thought. The hawk isn't moving. Is it dead? Jack stops and lifts the edge of his T-shirt.
The hawk's eyes are open and bright•.
It is alive•.
'Good boy,' says Jack.

When he arrives home he thinks of another problem. What can he do with the hawk?
'I can't take him into the house,' he thinks. 'My mum doesn't like cats and dogs. And she definitely doesn't like hawks! But I can't leave him outside all night.'
Then he has an idea. Jack walks round to the side of the house and opens the gate into the back garden. He quickly goes inside and closes the gate behind him.
He is in luck. The kitchen is dark. His parents are still in the living room. So he walks across the back garden. It only takes a moment. The garden is small. His parents only use it to store• old things they don't want. There is no grass or flowers. There are broken toys and tools• and lots of weeds and the perfect place to hide the hawk: the garden shed! He puts the hawk down on the floor with his T-shirt and closes the door behind him.

38

Jack's Endless Summer

Jack goes back to the front of the house and opens the door. It is late and he knows he is in big trouble•.
'Jack!' says his mother.
'I'm sorry, Mum, I – '
'Come in here at once!' she says. She pulls• him inside.
His father joins her in the hall.
'Why are you so late?' his father asks.
'Where's your T-shirt?' asks his mother.
'Erm... I...'
'Why can't you ring home, Jack?' asks his father.
'Where's your mobile?' adds his mother.
'I haven't got my mobile,' says Jack.
'Where is it?'
'I don't know.'
'You don't know? Mobile phones aren't toys, Jack! They're very expensive!' says his father. 'You're grounded•, Jack!' finishes his father. 'You aren't going out again for a week! Go to your room now!'
Jack walks past his parents and up the stairs. Jim watches him from the living room door.

39

Jack's Endless Summer

🎧 Jack sits at the kitchen table, watching his parents. He is waiting for them to leave for work.
'Remember, Jack, you can't go out.'
'I know,' Jack says. He doesn't want to go out. He wants to check Falco.
'And we don't want your friends here,' says his mother.
'Don't worry,' Jack says.
'You can play with your brother.'
'Yeah, OK,' says Jack. He looks at Jim. Jim is watching him.
After breakfast, Jim goes into the living room and plays video games. Jack waits at the table. When the front door clicks shut, he goes into the back garden. He is holding a small bowl• of water.
Nemo is sitting on the roof of the shed. Jack claps his hands.
'Go away! Go on, go!' he says.
Nemo doesn't move. Jack isn't happy. Nemo knows that a bird is inside.

Jack's Endless Summer

The shed is warm and dark inside. It takes a moment for Jack to see his T-shirt on the floor. Falco isn't on it. The bread is still on the floor next to it. But where is Falco?

It doesn't take Jack long to find him. The hawk is sitting quietly in a corner. Its eyes are open, but they aren't bright now. They are like clouds on a dull• day.

Jack puts the bowl of water in front of the hawk. At first, Falco ignores it. Then he dips• his beak into the water and drinks.

Jack sits quietly looking at the hawk. He remembers him flying above him in the endless blue sky. And now he is trapped on the earth. Jack wants to help him. But how?

Jack gets up and leaves the shed. When he is closing the door he looks up – Nemo is still sitting there on the roof!
'Go away, Nemo!' Jack says again. But Nemo ignores him.
Jack turns... and Jim is standing outside the kitchen door, waiting.
'What's Nemo doing wrong? Why can't he sit on the shed?' Jim asks.
'No reason,' says Jack.
'What's so interesting in the shed?'
'Nothing.'
Jim tries to pass Jack, but Jack blocks his way•.
'Tell me the truth, Jack. You're already in trouble with Mum and Dad.'
Jack thinks about this, but he doesn't think for long. He hasn't got any choice.
'Can you keep a secret, Jim?' he asks.
Jim likes secrets.
'You know I can. So let me see inside the shed.'

Jack's Endless Summer

They go back inside the shed and Jack introduces Jim to Falco.
'He's beautiful, Jack!'
'I know. But he isn't well. And he isn't getting better. Please don't say anything to Mum and Dad. I can mend• your rocket. Honest.'
'My rocket isn't important, Jack. Falco is. What's wrong with him?'
'He is injured• and he doesn't eat.'
'What do hawks eat?'
'Rabbits? Mice? I don't know. They don't eat bread, that's for sure.'
They stand in silence looking down at poor Falco.
Then Jack suddenly shouts out,
'Holly!'
Holly knows everything about animals and birds and nature.
Is she still on holiday?
Is she home? Jack hasn't got his mobile. He can't remember her message and he can't remember her phone number.
So Jack gets on his bike and cycles to her house.

Holly's house is on the other side of Westbourne. The houses are large and have garages and big gardens. Jack sees her house, jumps off his bike, runs up her path and rings the doorbell.
Holly opens the door. She sees a hot, red-faced• Jack.
'Jack! Are you all right?'
'I'm fine,' says Jack, 'I just want some information. Can you tell me about hawks?'
'Hawks? Why do you want to know?'
'I'm just interested, that's all. For example, what do they eat?'
In the afternoon, Jack and Jim take some meat from the fridge and cut it into very small pieces. They put it on a saucer• and go towards the shed. Nemo is immediately by their side, meowing and jumping up at the saucer. But they are prepared.
'Here you are, Nemo,' says Jim.
He puts a saucer of milk on the ground. And Nemo is purring• and happy at last!

Jack's Endless Summer

Over the next few days, Falco gets much better. He always eats the meat Jack and Jim bring him. Jack even digs up• worms• in the park and brings them home. Falco loves them! They disappear in seconds. His feathers look bright and shiny, too. Falco often opens his wings and beats them. But he can't fly. The shed is too small. And maybe his damaged• wing isn't strong.

Jack's parents are puzzled•. Every morning their two boys are nice to each other and they never argue.

'What's going on?' asks their mother. 'What are you two doing?'

'Nothing, Mum,' they say, and smile. She doesn't believe them. But what can she do?

Jack's Endless Summer

They open the door and step outside. Then they all wait.

Falco steps into the sunlight. He flaps his wings. Jack wants Falco to fly again, but he doesn't want him to go.

Nemo watches, too. But he doesn't jump down. This bird is big!

Beating his wings, Falco flies up into the air.

49

🎧 11 The hawk flies up into the big blue sky. He flies in small circles, then in large ones. Then suddenly he makes that familiar loud strange cry and flies away over the rooftops.
'It's a good thing, Jack,' says Jim.
'Falco can thank you for his new life,' says Holly.
Jack blinks• in the sunlight. He knows they are right. He agrees with them. But he can't say anything.
He stands and stares• up at the empty blue sky.

Jack's Endless Summer

Jack is soon free to go out and see his friends again.
They sit in the park.
They go swimming.
They play football.
And while they are walking around or hanging out, Jack sometimes sees Damian and his gang. Damian calls out, or throws a stone at him, but Jack ignores him. He isn't interested in Damian anymore. He isn't important. And Damian gets bored and forgets about Jack.
And all the time Jack is watching and waiting.
He is listening for a special sound.

Then one evening, Jack is sitting in his room looking out of the window. Jim is sitting on the bed playing with his rocket.
It is a cool evening at last. A light wind is blowing. Summer is finally coming to an end.
It is a quiet evening, too. For once, nobody is playing loud music. Jack can only hear the distant sound of the traffic on the ring road• around Westbourne.
Suddenly there is a noise in the back garden. Nemo jumps onto the fence•, looks up at the sky, and meows.
'What is he looking at?' thinks Jack.
And then he hears a distant cry. A strange cry. A familiar cry.

Jack's Endless Summer

A bird is flying in circles across the sky. Its black shape moves above the trees and houses.
Jack knows that shape. He knows that cry.
It is Falco.
He watches it fly, happy and wild and free.
Jack checks his mobile. He has one new message.

Hi Jack,
I'm back from Edinburgh! How RU?
Good summer?
David

Jack replies quickly, his eyes fixed on the hawk above his head.

Hi David,
A GREAT summer.
CU tomorrow.
I've got lots to tell u.
Jack

After Reading

Understanding the story

1 What happens in the story? Number the sentences in the correct order.

   a) ☐ Jack imagines he is flying above the town.
   b) ☐ Jack and Jim give the hawk meat and worms to eat.
   c) ☐ Damian jumps into the swimming pool next to Jack.
   d) ☐ Jack gets text messages from his friends on holiday.
   e) ☐ Jack sends David a text message.
   f) ☐ Jack hides the hawk in the garden shed.
   g) ☐ Jack breaks his brother's toy rocket.
   h) ☐ Jack asks Holly for help.
   i) ☐ Damian and his gang run after Jack.
   j) ☐ Jack carries the hawk home.

2 Write the names.

   a) .... is on holiday by the sea.
   b) .... is playing with his toys in the living room.
   c) .... and .... play Knock Down Ginger with Jack.
   d) .... hits the hawk with a stone from his catapult.
   e) Jack calls the hawk ....
   f) .... guesses Jack has a hawk and she wants to see it.

54

After Reading

3 What are the following? Why are they important? Tell a friend.

a)   b)   c)

d)   e)

4 Read the sentences then choose the correct word or words for each space.

a) That summer, Jack and his friends are very ....
   1 happy   2 bored   3 active

b) Jack always meets his friends ....
   1 at the shopping centre   2 at the swimming pool
   3 in the park

c) When Jack is under the tree, he imagines he is ....
   1 a shark   2 a horse   3 an action hero

d) Damian hits the hawk with a ....
   1 brick   2 rubber ball   3 stone

e) In the end, Falco flies away because he feels ....
   1 angry   2 better   3 sad

55

After Reading

Vocabulary

1 Match the actions with the pictures.

   1 to hide   **2** to climb   **3** to bounce   **4** to ring

   a)    b)

   c)    d)

2 Write a description of each picture.

   a) ....
   b) ....
   c) ....
   d) ....

3 Look at the pictures and ask and answer questions with a partner.

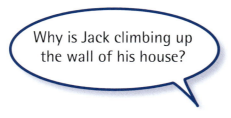

Why is Jack climbing up the wall of his house?

56

After Reading

4 When can you use these phrases? Match.

a) ☐ In a minute.
b) ☐ It's your fault.
c) ☐ Look out!
d) ☐ You're joking!
e) ☐ You're grounded.

1 You think another person is responsible.
2 You tell someone that they can't leave the house.
3 You don't want to do something immediately.
4 You think somebody isn't being serious.
5 You tell somebody to be careful.

5 Who says the phrases? Match then check in the story.

6 Complete the conversations with the phrases a–e above.

a) 'I want to go out.'
'Well, you can't. ....'

b) 'Can you help me with my homework?'
'OK, ...'

c) 'Oh no, Mum's angry!'
'....................
You're late.'

d) 'My sister is Johnny Depp's best friend.'
'....................'

e) '...................., there's a hole in the ground!'

57

After Reading

Grammar

Practise the Present Continuous

1 Look at the pictures. Complete the sentences using the verbs below.

worry   try   take   look   *lie*   follow

Jack .... on his bed.

Holly .... a photo of a cow.

Damian and his gang .... Jack.

Jack .... about the hawk.

The hawk .... to fly.

Jack .... out of the window.

Is it all right?

2 Write another sentence about each picture.

58

After Reading

Practise the Present Simple

3 Complete the sentences with the correct form of the verbs in the box.

> be   take off   (not) want   fly   feel   see

a) Jack .... his cap on the living room floor.
b) Jack and his friends .... very bored.
c) '............... you all right?' asks the pool attendant.
d) Jack .... his T-shirt and wraps it round the hawk.
e) The hawk .... to eat the pieces of bread.
f) In the end, the hawk .... up into the clear blue sky.

Practise short answers

4 Write short answers to these questions.

a) Is David on holiday in Switzerland?
....

b) Are Liam and Tareq Jack's friends?
....

c) Does Jack live in a big house?
....

d) Has Damian got a catapult?
....

e) Is Zadie lying on the beach?
....

f) Does Holly know a lot about animals?
....

After Reading

Exit Test

 1 Listen and tick (✓) the correct picture.

After Reading

2 Read the sentences about the story and choose the best word (1, 2 or 3) for each space.

a) Jack gets .... from his friends on holiday.
   1 postcards   **2** text messages   **3** emails

b) Jack breaks his brother's toy ....
   1 space station   **2** rocket   **3** astronaut

c) Jack imagines he is floating over the ....
   1 town   **2** swimming pool   **3** countryside

d) Jack finds the hawk behind a ....
   1 wooden box   **2** railway carriage   **3** big bush

e) Jack carries the hawk home inside his ....
   1 cap   **2** sweater   **3** T-shirt

f) Jack hides the hawk in ....
   1 his bedroom   **2** the back garden   **3** the shed

3 Look at the picture on page 32 of the story. Ask and answer questions about it.

- Who can you see in the picture?
- Where are they?
- What is happening?
- What happens next?

61

Glossary

1 **endless:** with no end; very long
11 **creeping:** moving slowly and quietly
12 **dim:** not light
   sticky: slightly wet so that it attaches to other surfaces
13 **breeze:** light wind
   loads: lots
14 **building:** structure with rooms, offices, apartments etc., inside
   floor: level in a building
   narrow: not wide
15 **picks up:** takes in his hand
   pity: (here) when you are sad about something
17 **fault:** responsibility; mistake
   stuff: things
18 **dust:** dry dirt in the form of a powder
   tarmac: black sticky substance for making road surfaces
   towards: in the direction of
19 **bounce:** hit a surface and move off it
   gutter: edge of the road where the water flows away
20 **annoyed:** a little angry
   enemy: someone who doesn't like you
   ignores: doesn't listen to
   RU: are you
   shark:
   sparkling: shining
23 **CU:** see you
   floating: staying up on the surface of water or in the air without moving
   spinning: moving round and round very fast
24 **coughing:** forcing water or air out of his mouth
   length: journey from one end of the pool to the other
25 **doesn't mean it:** is not sincere; is not really sorry
   edge: outside limit
   nods: moves his head up and down to say 'yes'
   pool attendant: someone whose job is to look after swimmers
   whistle:

Glossary

    wipes: (here) moves his hand over his eyes to remove the water
26 **repair:** fix
    soaps: TV serials about normal people
27 **ambush:** trap when you hide and catch people
    drifting: (here) floating
    imagines: forms a mental picture
    owl:

28 **doorbell:** something that makes a sound to let people know someone is at the door
29 **mates:** friends
31 **creep:** (here) unpleasant person
    definitely: certainly
32 **railway bridge:** structure to cross over a train track
33 **weeds:** wild plants
34 **bends down:** curves his body
    hang on: wait
35 **fires:** shoots; sends
    good shot: well hit
    swoops: moves quickly through the air
36 **bushes:** type of small, fat tree
    hoot: make the sound typical of owls
    in pain: suffering physically
    screeches: makes a loud high noise
37 **alive:** living; not dead
    bright: shiny
    wraps: (here) puts
38 **store:** keep
    tools: instruments
39 **is in big trouble:** has a lot of problems
    grounded: not allowed to leave the house
    pulls: (here) moves him towards her
42 **bowl:** dish
43 **dips:** (here) puts
    dull: not bright
44 **blocks his way:** stops him from passing
45 **injured:** hurt; physically harmed

46 **purring:** making the sound a cat makes when it's happy
   red-faced: with a red face
   saucer: small plate that goes under a cup
47 **damaged:** injured; broken
   digs up: gets out of the earth
   puzzled: confused; don't understand
   worms:

50 **blinks:** opens and closes his eyes
   stares: looks for a long time
52 **fence:**

   ring road: main road around the edge of a town